Quilt Us
a Rock!

Written by Judy Bruns

Illustrated by Renee Robinson

Published in 2019, by Coco Publications

Coldwater, OH 45828

Copyright @ Judy Bruns

Bruns, Judy

Quilt Us a Rock!

Story by Judy Bruns / Illustrations by Renee Robinson

ISBN
978-0-971-39264-1

Library of Congress Control Number:
2019906605

Edited by Judy Bruns
Book Design by Renee Robinson

PRINTED IN THE UNITED STATES OF AMERICA

Dedication Page

Thank you, Brenda Robinson, for your inspiration in transforming
a rock into a story! — J.B.

For the wonderful woman who inspired this story, the one who
made it all happen, the one and only Brenda Robinson, my mom! — R.R.

"Mom, how long?"

"We're coming up to the big rock,
so what does that tell you, Renee?"

"It won't be long till we get to school."

"That's right!"

The big rock has been as good as a road sign for our family.
It helps other people, too. It gets them where they want to go.

Aunt Linda once said, "I know I'm on the right road,
or the wrong one, because of that rock!"

We have fun with the rock, too. Sometimes when we go by it, we pretend the rock is a

MONSTER.

Or a

MOUNTAIN.

Or a

VISITOR FROM MARS.

Katlin says, "It's just a big rock, you sillies!"

But my brother Nathan insists, "It's a dinosaur!"

"Well, I guess it's about as tall and heavy as some dinosaurs," Mom says.

"When the stone quarry company moved it here to hold up their sign, they had to use giant machines. I've heard that it is 15 feet tall. Think of 4 Ashleys stacked on top of each other," Mom laughs. "That's how high it is. How heavy do you think it is?"

"5,000 pounds!" I blurt out.

Nathan shakes his head and shouts, "It's more!"

"You're right, Nathan," Mom says. "The men who moved the rock say it weighs 30 tons."

$$2,000 \text{ LBS} = 1 \text{ TON}$$

$$2,000 \times 30 = 60,000$$

Katlin figures, "There are 2,000 pounds in a ton. Take 2,000 times 30, and that equals 60,000 pounds. Wow!"

That rock is amazing to my sisters and brothers and me. We stare at it every time we pass by.

But today,

something is different. . .

Words are painted on it. Some of them are bad words. They are dripping down the sides of our rock.

As time goes on, we see more words. Mom calls it "graffiti." We all call it a "mess."

"One of these days," Mom says, **_"I'm going to paint that rock!"_**

Oh no! I'm thinking. *She's going to write more graffiti!* But when Mom makes up her mind to do something, you can't stop her.

Mom asks us kids to name our favorite colors.

Little John says, "Orange!"

Ashley's favorite is, "Yellow!"

Nathan's is, "Red!"

Katlin says, "Blue,"

and I say, "Green!"

"Why do you want to know, Mom?" we ask... She just smiles.

"Your Great-Grandma Alvera taught me how to quilt, Renee."
"Are you going to make us a quilt?" asks Ashley.
"I could never be as great a quilter as Great-Grandma is. . .

But, I know something I *can* do!"

"What's that?" Little John, usually quiet, wants to know.

Mom announces, to our surprise,
                "I'm going to *quilt us a rock!*"

Now, Mom is the quiet one the rest of the way home. She's got us wondering. *What is she up to?*

We walk into the house, and Mom finally speaks.
"Katlin, I need you to babysit. I'll be right back."

"Sure," my sister replies. "Where are you going?"
But Mom has already rushed out the door.

An hour later, Mom comes in the door with cans of paint and paint brushes!

I'm thinking, **She's really going to do it!**

In the morning, we drive a different way to school.

In the afternoon, we come home that same way.

We tell Mom about our day, and she tells us about hers. This goes on for a couple weeks as she drives us home from school. As I listen, I get pictures in my head.

She paints
the bottom of
the rock.

She paints
the middle of
the rock.

And she climbs HIGH up on a ladder to paint the top. My Aunt Linda holds the ladder steady for her.

We see paint under her fingernails and in her hair for what seems like *forever*.

Then at Friday's supper table we hear, "Would you like to see the rock in the morning?"

Heads nod up and down. Nathan is so excited that he almost falls off his chair!

We'll get to see her. . .graffiti? I wonder.

Morning comes. We jump into the van and take off.
The closer we get, the more excited we become!

Then we see it. One of
Great-Grandma's quilts
is hanging from the sky!

Wait! **It's the rock!** Our mouths and eyes
open wide in surprise!

What used to be a mess is now painted with
beautiful squares of our *favorite* colors. Best of all,
the graffiti is gone!

Mom parks the van, and everyone piles out. We run to the rock
to stare at it close-up. Then we look it over, up and down and all around.

"I want each of you to sign your name and your age on the rock," Mom says. And we do—even Little John, with some help.

Renee Robinson
age 11

Kalin R.

John
im 5yr.

Ashley R
7 2007

Today, cars and school buses go by our rock.
The drivers know how far they have to go yet and where to turn.

Truck drivers do, too!

A reporter comes out to take our picture.

WE'RE IN THE NEWSPAPER!

And the stone quarry people are happy that Mom asked to paint their rock. It gets their Stoneco sign a lot of good attention!

My mom has kept her promise. **She said she would
quilt us a rock. And she *did*.**

AUTHOR'S NOTE

In 1971, the John W. Karch Stone Company had a 15-foot tall, 30-ton rock moved to Route 29 west of Celina, Ohio, to advertise their stone quarry, Stoneco. But people of the area became upset when, over time, graffiti covered it. In 2007 Brenda Robinson changed all of that. After getting permission from the stone quarry company, she painted the rock with her children's favorite colors. Her quilting grandma was her inspiration. Now the Quilted Rock of Mercer County is a landmark for travelers, truckers, and for cars and buses of children on their way to school.

ILLUSTRATOR'S NOTE

The painter of the Quilted Rock, Brenda Robinson, tackles challenging projects, and they often end up being "attractions" in area communities—from the enormous "Big Bob" fish float at the annual Celina, Ohio Lake Festival, to the Santa house that sits each Christmas season on the Mercer County Courthouse lawn. Her large, homemade wooden signs decorate yards throughout the region, especially during the holidays. Brenda Robinson always has a new project in the works. She's an energetic, unstoppable woman, and I say proudly that she's my mom.

R.I.P.

Alvera E. Stucke
The "quilter" who inspired the "painter."

ABOUT THE AUTHOR

Judy Bruns holds degrees in education and guidance counseling. She has taught creative writing and has coached local Power of the Pen teams. Bruns is a wife, a mother, a grandmother, and an ardent volunteer for causes close to her heart. *Quilt Us a Rock!* is her 8th children's picture book. She has also authored a book for middle school teachers on narrative writing and a book of 82 short stories and poems for adults, besides numerous freelance articles for newspapers and magazines.

Children's picture books by Judy Bruns:

- Thousand Dollar Baseball
- Painting Grandma's Nails
- Billy Joe Boomershine and the Toilet Paper Bandit
- Now I'm a BIG Girl!
- Now I'm a BIG Boy!
- Hattie and Her 43 Cats
- Donnie, Lost in the Cornfield

Other books by Judy Bruns:

- Rhymes & Ramblings of a Small Town Girl
- Prompts That Make Kids BEG To Write!
  (200 writing prompts)

ABOUT THE ILLUSTRATOR

Renee Robinson holds a degree in graphic design with a concentration in illustration from the University of Saint Francis, Fort Wayne, Indiana. She has been given several awards through the Fort Wayne Advertising Honors, which include three Gold Awards and two Silver Awards. While in school, she served as the American Advertising Federation (AAF) club president and a First Year Experience club leader. As the president of AAF, Renee also served as a student representative on the Fort Wayne AdFed Board. She hopes to continue using her illustration and design skills to help others reach their goals.

Not only is this Renee's first illustrated book, but it is also a story dear to her heart. And yes, *Quilt Us a Rock* is told from her perspective. She is "Renee."

CPSIA information can be obtained
at www.ICGtesting.com
Printed in the USA
LVIC061718040919
629920LV00004B/44

* 9 7 8 0 9 7 1 3 9 2 6 4 9 *